RAINBOW magic ®

The Rainbow Fairies

Dedicated to Fiona Waters,
who has loved fairies
all her life

Special thanks to
Narinder Dhami

ORCHARD BOOKS
338 Euston Road, London NW1 3BH
Orchard Books Australia
Level 17/207 Kent Street, Sydney, NSW 2000
A Paperback Original

First published in 2003 by Orchard Books.

HiT entertainment

Illustrations © Georgie Ripper 2003

A CIP catalogue record for this book is available
from the British Library.

ISBN 978 1 84362 017 4
50

Printed in Great Britain

Orchard Books is a division of Hachette Children's Books,
an Hachette Livre UK company

www.hachettelivre.co.uk

Amber
the Orange Fairy

by Daisy Meadows

illustrated by Georgie Ripper

ORCHARD

Jack Frost's
Ice Castle

Tom Goodfellow's
House

Merry-go-round

Willow
Tree

Mrs Merry's
Cottage

Stream

Field

Mermaid
Cottage

Town

Harbour

Dolphin Cottage

Cold winds blow and thick ice form,
I conjure up this fairy storm.
To seven corners of the mortal world
the Rainbow Fairies will be hurled!

I curse every part of Fairyland,
with a frosty wave of my icy hand.
For now and always, from this fateful day,
Fairyland will be cold and grey!

Ruby is safely hidden in the pot-at-the-end-of-the-rainbow. Now Rachel and Kirsty must find
Amber the Orange Fairy.

Contents

A Very Unusual Shell   9

The Magic Feather   21

A Stranger in the Pot   31

Home Sweet Home   41

Goblin Alert!   59

Bertram to the Rescue   67

A Very Unusual Shell

"What a lovely day!" Rachel Walker shouted, staring up at the blue sky. She and her friend, Kirsty Tate, were running along Rainspell Island's yellow, sandy beach. Their parents walked a little way behind them.

"It's a *magical* day," Kirsty added. The two friends smiled at each other.

Rachel and Kirsty had come to
Rainspell Island for their holidays.
They had soon found out it really *was* a
magical place!

As they ran, they passed rock pools
that shone like jewels in the sunshine.

Rachel spotted a little *splash!* in one
of the pools. "There's something in
there, Kirsty!" she pointed. "Let's go and
look."

The girls jogged over to the pool and
crouched down to see.

Kirsty's heart thumped as she gazed into the crystal clear water. "What is it?" she asked.

Suddenly, the water rippled. A little brown crab scuttled sideways across the sandy bottom and vanished under a rock.

Kirsty felt disappointed. "I thought it might be another Rainbow Fairy," she said.

"So did I, "Rachel sighed. "Never mind. We'll keep on looking."

"Of course we will," Kirsty agreed. Then she put her finger to her lips as their parents came up behind them. "*Ssh.*"

Kirsty and Rachel had a big secret. They were helping to find the Rainbow Fairies. Thanks to Jack Frost's wicked spell, the fairies were lost on Rainspell Island. And until they were all found there would be no colour in Fairyland.

Rachel looked at the shimmering blue sea. "Shall we have a swim?" she asked.

But Kirsty wasn't listening. She was shading her eyes with her hand and looking further along the beach. "Over there, Rachel – by those rocks," she said.

Then Rachel could see it too – something winking and sparkling in the sunshine. "Wait for me!" she called, as Kirsty hurried over there.

When they saw what it was, the two
friends sighed in disappointment.

"It's just the wrapper from a
chocolate bar," Rachel said sadly. She
bent down and picked up the shiny
purple foil.

Kirsty thought for a moment. "Do you remember what the Fairy Queen said?" she asked.

Rachel nodded. "*Let my magic come to you,*" she said. "You're right, Kirsty. We should just enjoy our holiday, and wait for the magic to happen. After all, that's how we found Ruby in the pot-at-the-end-of-the-rainbow, isn't it?" She put down her beach bag on the sand. "Come on – race you into the sea!"

They rushed into the water. The sea was cold and salty, but the sun felt warm on their backs. They waved at their parents, sitting on the sand, and splashed about in the waves until they got goosebumps.

"Ow!" Kirsty gasped as they paddled out of the water. "I just stood on something sharp."

"It might have been a shell," said Rachel. "There are lots of them round here." She picked up a pale pink one and showed it to Kirsty.

"Let's see how many we can find," Kirsty said.

The two girls walked along the beach looking for shells. They found long, thin, blue shells and tiny, round, white shells.

Soon their hands were full. They had
walked right round the curve of the bay.
Rachel looked over her shoulder and
a sudden gust of wind whipped her
hair across her face.
"Look how far we've
come," she said.
Kirsty stopped. The
wind tugged at her
T-shirt and made
goosebumps stand
out on her arms.
"It's getting cold
now," she said.
"Shall we
go back?"
"Yes, it must be
nearly teatime,"
said Rachel.

The two girls began to walk back along the beach. They'd only gone a few steps when the wind suddenly dropped again.

"That's funny," said Kirsty. "It's not windy here."

They looked back and saw little swirls of sand being blown in the wind where they'd just been. "Oh!" said Rachel, and the two friends looked at each other with excitement.

"It's magic," Kirsty whispered. "It *has* to be!"

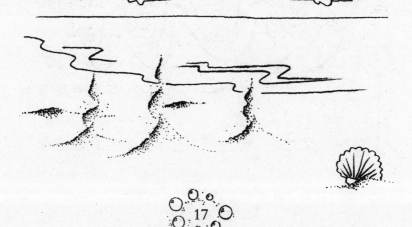

They walked back and the breeze swirled around their legs again. Then the golden sand at their feet began to drift gently to one side, as if invisible hands were pushing it away. A large scallop shell appeared, much bigger than the other shells on the beach. It was pearly white with soft orange streaks, and it was tightly closed.

Quickly the girls knelt down on the sand, spilling the little shells out of their hands. Kirsty was just about to pick up the scallop shell when Rachel put out her hand. "Listen," she whispered.

They both listened hard.

There it was again.

Inside the shell, a tiny, silvery voice hummed softly...

The Magic Feather

Very carefully, Rachel picked up the
shell. It felt warm and smooth.

The humming stopped
at once. "I mustn't be
scared," said the tiny
voice. "I just have to
be brave, and help will
come very soon."

Hummm....

Kirsty put her face close to the shell. "Hello," she whispered. "Is there a fairy in there?"

"Yes!" cried the voice. "I'm Amber the *Orange* Fairy! Can you get me out of here?"

"Of course we will," Kirsty promised. "My name is Kirsty, and my friend Rachel is here too." She looked up at Rachel, her eyes shining.

"We've found another Rainbow Fairy!"

"Quick," Rachel said. "Let's get the shell open." She took hold of the scallop shell and tried to pull the two halves apart. Nothing happened.

"Try again," said
Kirsty. She and Rachel
each grasped one half
of the shell and tugged.
But the shell stayed
tightly shut.

"What's happening?"
Amber called. She sounded worried.

"We can't open the shell," Kirsty said.
"But we'll think of something." She
turned to Rachel. "If we find a piece of
driftwood, maybe we could use it to
open the shell."

Rachel glanced around the beach.
"I can't see any driftwood," she said.
"We could try tapping the shell
on a rock."

"But that might hurt Amber," Kirsty
pointed out.

Suddenly Rachel remembered
something. "What about the magic bags
the Fairy Queen gave us?" she said.

"Of course!" Kirsty cried. She put
her face close to the shell again.
"Amber, we're going to
look in our magic
bags," she said.
"OK, but please
hurry," Amber called.
Rachel opened her
beach bag. The two
magic bags were hidden
under her towel. One of the bags
was glowing with a golden light.
Carefully, Rachel pulled it out.
"Look," she whispered to Kirsty. "This
one is all lit up."

"Open it, quick," Kirsty whispered back.

As Rachel undid the bag, a fountain of glittering sparks flew out.

"What's inside?" Kirsty asked, her eyes wide.

Rachel slid her hand into the bag. She could feel something light and soft. She pulled it out, scattering sparkles everywhere.

It was a shimmering golden feather.

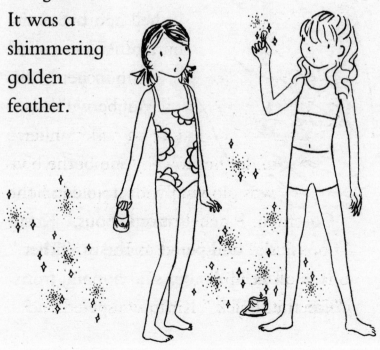

Kirsty and Rachel stared at the feather.

"It's really pretty," said Kirsty. "But what are we going to *do* with it?"

"I don't know," Rachel replied. She tried to use the feather to push the two halves of the shell apart. But the feather just curled up in her hand. "Maybe we should ask Amber."

"Amber, we've looked in the magic bags," Kirsty said, "and we've found a feather."

"Oh, good!" Amber said happily from inside the shell.

"But we don't know what to do with it," Rachel added.

Amber laughed. It sounded like the tinkle of a tiny bell. "You tickle the shell, of course!" she said.

"Do you think that will work?" Rachel said to Kirsty.

"Let's give it a try," Kirsty said.

Rachel began to tickle the shell with the feather. At first nothing happened. Then they heard a soft, gritty chuckle. Then another and another. Slowly the two halves of the shell began to open.

"It's working," Kirsty gasped. "Keep tickling, Rachel!"

The shell was laughing hard now. The two halves opened wider...

And there, sitting inside the smooth, peach-coloured shell, was Amber the Orange Fairy.

A Stranger in the Pot

"I'm free!" Amber cried joyfully.

She shot out of the shell and up into the air, her wings fluttering in a rainbow-coloured blur. Orange fairy dust floated down around Kirsty and Rachel. It turned into orange bubbles as it fell. One of the bubbles landed on Rachel's arm and burst with a tiny POP!

"The bubbles smell like oranges!"
Rachel smiled.

Amber spun through the sky, turning
cartwheels one after the other. "Thank
you!" she called. Then she swooped
down towards Rachel and Kirsty.

She wore a shiny orange catsuit and
long boots. Her flame-coloured hair was
held in a high ponytail, tied with a band
of peach blossoms. In her hand was an
orange wand tipped with gold.

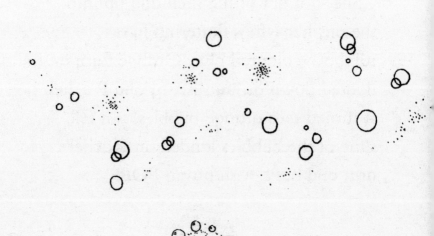

"I'm so glad you found me!" Amber
shouted. She landed on Rachel's
shoulder, then cartwheeled lightly across
to Kirsty's. "But who are you? And
where are my Rainbow sisters? And
what's happening in Fairyland? How am
I going to get back there?"

Kirsty and Rachel couldn't get a
word in.

Suddenly, Amber stopped. She floated
down and landed softly on Rachel's hand.
"I'm sorry," she said with a smile. "But I
haven't had anyone to talk to. I've been
shut up in this shell ever since Jack Frost's
spell banished us from Fairyland. How did
you know where to find me?"

"Kirsty and I promised your sister Ruby
that we would look for all the Rainbow
Fairies," Rachel told her.

"Ruby?" Amber's face lit up. She spun
round on Rachel's hand. "You've found
Ruby?"

"Yes, she's quite safe," Rachel said.
"She's in the pot-at-the-end-of-the-
rainbow."

Amber did a joyful backflip. "Please
take me to her!" she begged.

"I'll ask our parents if we can go for

a walk," Kirsty said. And she ran off across the beach.

"Do you know what is happening in Fairyland?" Amber asked Rachel.

Rachel nodded. She and Kirsty had flown with Ruby to Fairyland. Ruby had shrunk them to fairy size and given them fairy wings.  "King Oberon and Queen Titania miss you very much," Rachel told Amber. "With no colour, Fairyland is a sad place."

Amber's wing drooped.

Kirsty was hurrying back towards
them. "Mum said we can go for a
walk," she panted.

"Well, what are we waiting for? Let's
go!" Amber called. She flew up and
did a somersault in mid-air.
Rachel pulled their shorts,
T-shirts and trainers
out of her beach
bag and both girls
put them on.
"Rachel, could
you bring my
shell?" Amber asked.
Rachel looked surprised.
"Yes, if you want," she said.
Amber nodded. "It's really comfy," she
explained. "It will make a lovely bed for
me and my sisters."

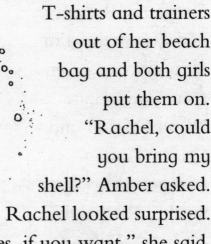

Rachel put the shell in her beach bag, and they set off, with Amber sitting cross-legged on Kirsty's shoulder.

"My wings are a bit stiff after being in the shell," she told them. "I don't think I can fly very far yet."

The girls followed the path to the
clearing in the wood where the pot-at-
the-end-of-the-rainbow was hidden.

"Here we are," said Rachel. "The pot
is over there." She stopped. The pot was
where they'd left it, under the weeping
willow tree. But climbing out of it was a
big, green frog.

"Oh no!" Rachel gasped. She and Kirsty stared at the frog in horror.

Where was Ruby?

Home Sweet Home

Rachel dashed forward and grabbed the frog round his plump, green tummy.

The frog turned his head and glared at her, his eyes bulging. "And what do you think *you're* doing?" he croaked.

Rachel was so shocked, she let go of the frog. He hopped away from her, looking very annoyed.

"It's a talking frog!" Kirsty gasped, her eyes wide. "And it looks like it's wearing glasses..."

"Bertram!" Amber flew down from Kirsty's shoulder. "I didn't know it was you."

Bertram bowed his head as Amber hugged him. "Thank goodness you're safe, Miss Amber!" he said happily. "And may I say, it's very good to see you again."

Amber beamed at Rachel and Kirsty.
"Bertram isn't an ordinary frog, you
know," she explained. "He's one of King
Oberon's footmen."

"Oh, yes!" said
Kirsty. "I remember
now. We saw the
frog footmen
when we went
to Fairyland
with Ruby."

"But they were
wearing purple
uniforms then," Rachel added.

"Excuse me, Miss, but a frog in a
purple uniform would *not* be a good
idea on Rainspell Island," Bertram
pointed out. "It's much better if I look
like an ordinary frog."

"But what are you doing here, Bertram?" asked Amber. "And where's Ruby?"

"Don't worry, Miss Amber," Bertram replied. "Miss Ruby is safe in the pot." He suddenly looked very stern. "King Oberon sent me to Rainspell. The Cloud Fairies spotted Jack Frost's goblins sneaking out of Fairyland. We think he has sent them here to stop the Rainbow Fairies being found."

Kirsty felt a shiver run down her spine. "Jack Frost's goblins?" she said.

"They're his servants," Amber explained. Her wings trembled and she looked very scared. "They'd rather keep Fairyland cold and grey!"

"Never fear, Miss Amber," Bertram croaked. "I'll look after you."

Suddenly a shower of red fairy dust shot out of the pot. Ruby fluttered out. "I heard voices," she shouted joyfully. "Amber! I *knew* it was you!"

"Ruby!" Amber called. And she cartwheeled through the air towards her sister.

Rachel and Kirsty watched as the two fairies flew into each other's arms. The air around them fizzed with tiny red flowers and orange bubbles.

"Thank you, Kirsty and Rachel," said Ruby. She and Amber floated down to them, holding hands. "It's so good to have Amber back safely."

"What about you?" Rachel asked. "Have you been all right in the pot?"

Ruby nodded. "I'm fine now that Bertram is here," she replied. "And I've been making the pot into a fairy home."

"I've brought my shell with me," Amber said. "It will make a lovely bed for us. Show her, Rachel."

Rachel put her bag down on the grass and took the creamy orange shell out of it.

"It's beautiful," said Ruby. Then she smiled at Rachel and Kirsty. "Would you like to come and see our new home?" she asked.

"But the pot's too small for Kirsty and me to get inside," Rachel began. Then she began to tingle with excitement. "Are you going to make us fairy size again?"

Ruby nodded. She and Amber flew over the girls' heads, showering them with fairy dust. Rachel and Kirsty started to shrink, just as they had done before. Soon they were tiny, the same size as Ruby and Amber.

"I *love* being a fairy," Kirsty said happily. She twisted round to look at her silvery wings.

"Me too," Rachel agreed. She was getting used to seeing flowers as tall as trees!

Bertram hopped over to the pot. "I'll wait outside," he croaked.

"Come this way," said Ruby. She took Rachel's hand, and Amber took Kirsty's. Then the fairies led them towards the pot.

Rachel and Kirsty fluttered through the air, dodging a butterfly that was as big as they were. Its wings felt like velvet as they brushed gently past it.

"I'm getting better at flying!" Kirsty laughed as she landed neatly on the edge of the pot. She looked down eagerly.

The pot was full of sunlight. There were little chairs made from twigs tied with blades of grass. Each chair had a cushion made from a soft red berry. Rugs of bright green leaves covered the floor.

"Shall we bring in the shell?" asked Rachel.

The others thought this was a very good idea. When they flew out of the pot, Bertram was already pushing the shell across the grass towards them.

"Here you are," he croaked.

The shell seemed very heavy now that
Rachel and Kirsty were the same size as
Ruby and Amber. But Bertram helped
them to heave it into the pot.

Soon the shell bed was
placed neatly inside.
Ruby lined it with
sweet-smelling
rose petals.

"The pot looks
lovely," Rachel said.

"I wish I could live
here too!" said Kirsty.

Ruby turned to her sister.
"Do like it, Amber?" she asked.

"It's beautiful," Amber replied. "It
reminds me of our house back in
Fairyland. I wish I could see Fairyland
again. I miss it so much."

Ruby smiled. "Well, I can show you Fairyland," she said, "even though we can't go back there yet. Follow me."

Bertram was still on guard next to the pot when they flew out again. "Where are you going, Miss Ruby?" he croaked.

"To the magic pond," Ruby replied. "Come with us." She sprinkled her magic dust over Rachel and Kirsty. Quickly they grew back to their normal size.

They went over to the pond. Ruby flew above the water, scattering fairy dust. Just as before, a picture began to appear. "Fairyland!" Amber cried, gazing into the water. Rachel and Kirsty watched too. Fairyland still looked sad and chilly. The palace, the toadstool houses, the flowers and the trees were all drab and grey.

Suddenly a cold breeze rippled the
surface of the water, and the picture
began to fade.

"What's happening?" Kirsty whispered.
Everyone stared down at the pond.

Another picture was taking shape – a
thin, grinning face with frosty white hair
and icicles hanging from his beard.

"Jack Frost!" Ruby gasped in horror.
As she spoke, the air turned icy cold and
the edges of the pool began to freeze.

"What's happening?" Rachel asked, shivering.

Bertram hopped forward. "This is bad news," he said. "It means that Jack Frost's goblins are close by!"

Goblin Alert!

Rachel and Kirsty felt shivers run down
their spine as the whole pond froze over.
Jack Frost's grinning face faded away.

"Follow me," ordered Bertram. He
hopped over to a large bush. "We'll hide
here."

"Maybe we should go back to the pot,"
said Ruby.

"Not if the goblins are close by,"
Bertram replied. "We mustn't let them
know where the pot is."

The two girls crouched down behind
the bush next to Bertram. Ruby and
Amber sat very still on Kirsty's shoulder.
It was getting colder and colder. Rachel
and Kirsty couldn't stop their teeth
chattering.

"What are the goblins like?" Rachel
asked.

"They're bigger than us," said Amber.
She was trembling with fright.

"And they have ugly faces and hooked
noses and big feet," Ruby added,
holding her sister's hand for
comfort.

"Hush, Miss Ruby,"
Bertram croaked. "I
can hear something."

Rachel and Kirsty
listened. Suddenly,
Rachel saw a hook-nosed
shadow flit across the clearing
towards them. She grabbed Kirsty's arm.
They were peering out of the bush when
the leaves rustled right next to them.
They almost jumped out of their skin.

"Oi!" said a gruff voice, sounding very close. "What do you think you're doing?"

Rachel and Kirsty held their breath.

"Nothing," said another gruff voice, very rudely.

"Goblins!" Amber whispered nervously in Kirsty's ear.

"You stood on my toe," said the first goblin crossly.

"No, I didn't," snapped the other goblin.

"Yes, you did! Keep your big feet to yourself!"

"Well, at least my nose isn't as big as yours!"

The bush shook even more. It sounded as if the goblins were pushing and shoving each other.

"Get out of my way!" one of them shouted. "Ow!"

"That'll teach you to push *me*!" yelled the other one.

Rachel and Kirsty looked at each other in alarm. What if the goblins found them there?

"Come on," puffed one of the goblins. "Jack Frost will be really cross if we don't find these fairies. You know he wants us to stop them getting back to Fairyland."

"Well, they're not here, are they?" grumbled the other. "Let's try somewhere else."

The voices died away. The leaves stopped rustling. And suddenly the air felt warm again. There was a cracking sound as the frozen pond began to melt.

"They've gone," Bertram croaked. "Quick, we must get back to the pot."

They all hurried across the clearing. The pot stood under the weeping willow tree, just as before.

"I'll stay outside in case the goblins
come back," Bertram began. But a shout
from Kirsty stopped them all in their
tracks.

"Look!" she cried. "The pot's frozen
over!"

Kirsty was right. The top of the pot was
covered with a thick sheet of ice. No one,
not even a fairy, could get inside.

Bertram to the Rescue

"Oh no!" Ruby gasped. "The goblins must have passed really close. Thank goodness they didn't discover the pot."

She flew over to the pot with Amber right behind her. They drummed on the ice with their tiny fists. But it was too thick for them to break through.

"Shall we try, Rachel?" asked Kirsty. "Maybe we could smash the ice with a stick."

But Bertram had another idea. "Stand back, please, everyone," he said.

The girls moved to the edge of the clearing. Ruby sat on Kirsty's hand, and Amber flew over to Rachel. They all watched.

Suddenly, Bertram leaped forward with a mighty hop. He jumped straight at the sheet of ice, kicking out with his webbed feet. But the ice did not break.

"Let's try again," he panted.

He jumped forward
again and hit the ice.
This time, there was a
loud cracking sound.
One more jump, and
the ice shattered into
little pieces. Some of it
fell inside the pot. Rachel
and Kirsty rushed over to fish
out these bits before they melted.

"There you are," Bertram croaked.

"Thank you, Bertram," Ruby called.
She and Amber flew down and hugged
the frog.

Bertram looked pleased. "Just doing
my job, Miss Ruby," he said. "You and
Miss Amber must stay very close to the
pot from now on. It's dangerous for you
to go too far."

"We've got to say
goodbye to our friends
first," Amber told him. She
flew into the air and did a
backflip, smiling at Rachel
and Kirsty. "Thank you a
thousand times."

"We'll see you again soon," said
Rachel.

"When we've found your next
Rainbow sister," Kirsty added.

"Good luck!" said Ruby. "We'll be
waiting here for you. Come on, Amber."

She took her sister's hand, and
they flew over to the pot.
The two fairies turned
around to wave at the girls.
Then they disappeared
inside.

"Don't worry," Bertram said. "I'll look after them."

"We know you will," Rachel said, as she picked up her beach bag. She and Kirsty walked out of the wood. "I'm glad Ruby isn't on her own any more," said Rachel. "Now she's got Amber *and* Bertram."

"I didn't like those goblins," Kirsty said with a shudder. "I hope they don't come back again."

They made their way back to the beach. Their parents were packing away their towels. Rachel's dad saw Rachel and Kirsty coming down the lane and went to meet them. "You've been a long time," he smiled. "We were just coming to look for you."

"Are we going home now?" Rachel asked.

Mr Walker nodded. "It's very strange," he said. "It's suddenly turned quite chilly."

As he spoke, a cold breeze swirled around Rachel and Kirsty. They shivered and looked up at the sky. The sun had disappeared behind a thick, black cloud. The trees swayed in the wind, and the leaves rustled as if they were whispering to each other.

"Jack Frost's goblins are still here!" Kirsty gasped.

"You're right," Rachel agreed. "Let's hope Bertram can keep Ruby and Amber safe while we look for the other Rainbow Fairies."

Now it's time for Kirsty and Rachel to help...

Saffron the Yellow Fairy

Read on for a sneak peek...

"Over here, Kirsty!" called Rachel Walker. Kirsty ran down one of the emerald green fields that covered this part of Rainspell Island. Buttercups and daisies dotted the grass.

"Don't go too far!" Kirsty's mum called. She and Kirsty's dad were climbing over a stile at the top of the field.

Kirsty caught up with her friend. "What have you found, Rachel? Is it another Rainbow Fairy?" she asked hopefully.

"I don't know." Rachel was standing on the bank of a rippling stream. "I thought I heard something."

Kirsty's face lit up. "Maybe there's a fairy in the stream?"

Rachel nodded. She knelt down on the soft grass and put her ear close to the water.

Kirsty crouched down too, and listened really hard.

The sun glittered on the water as it splashed over big, shiny pebbles. Tiny rainbows flashed and sparkled – red, orange, yellow, green, blue, indigo, and violet.

And then they heard a tiny bubbling voice. "Follow me..." it gurgled. "Follow me..."

"Oh!" Rachel gasped. "Did you hear that?"

"Yes," said Kirsty, her eyes wide. "It must be a *magic* stream!"

Rachel felt her heart beat fast. "Maybe the stream will lead us to the Yellow Fairy," she said.

Rachel and Kirsty had a special secret. They had promised the King and Queen of Fairyland they would find the lost Rainbow Fairies. Jack Frost's spell had hidden the Rainbow Fairies on Rainspell Island. Fairyland would be cold and grey until all seven fairies had been found and returned to their home...

Read Saffron the Yellow Fairy to find out what adventures are in store for Kirsty and Rachel!

Meet the
Rainbow Fairies

Ruby
the Red
Fairy

Amber
the Orange
Fairy

Saffron
the Yellow
Fairy

Fern
the Green
Fairy

Sky
the Blue
Fairy

Izzy
the Indigo
Fairy

Heather
the Violet
Fairy

Also available
as an ebook

Collect the seven original Rainbow Magic Fairies
to find out how the adventure began!

www.rainbowmagicbooks.co.uk

Meet the fairies, play games
and get sneak peeks at
the latest books!

There's fairy fun for everyone at

www.rainbowmagicbooks.co.uk

You'll find great activities, competitions, stories and
fairy profiles, and also a special newsletter.

Win Rainbow Magic Goodies!

There are lots of Rainbow Magic fairies, and we want to know which one is your favourite! Send us a picture of her and tell us in thirty words why she is your favourite and why you like Rainbow Magic books. Each month we will put the entries into a draw and select one winner to receive a Rainbow Magic Sparkly T-shirt and Goody Bag!

Send your entry on a postcard to Rainbow Magic Competition, Orchard Books, 338 Euston Road, London NW1 3BH.
Australian readers should email: childrens.books@hachette.com.au
New Zealand readers should write to Rainbow Magic Competition, PO Box 3255, Shortland St, Auckland 1140, NZ.
Don't forget to include your name and address.
Only one entry per child.

Good luck!

Meet the
Weather Fairies

Crystal
the Snow
Fairy

Abigail
the Breeze
Fairy

Pearl
the Cloud
Fairy

Goldie
the Sunshine
Fairy

Evie
the Mist
Fairy

Storm
the Lightning
Fairy

Hayley
the Rain
Fairy

Join Rachel and Kirsty as they hunt for the
feathers that naughty Jack Frost has stolen
from Doodle the magic weather-vane cockerel!

www.rainbowmagicbooks.co.uk